D1443762

SUMMER COAT, WINTER COAT

The Story of a Snowshoe Hare

SMITHSONIAN
WILD HERITAGE COLLECTION

For Lorraine, my sister, and Lorraine,
my friend, with love and gratitude
— D.B.

To my wife, Carol, and son, Matthew,
who keep me in line
— A.D.

Copyright © 1993 by Trudy Management Corporation,
165 Water Street, Norwalk, CT 06856, and the Smithsonian Institution,
Washington, DC 20560.

Book Design: Johanna P. Shields

First Edition
10 9 8 7 6 5 4 3 2 1
Printed in Singapore

Library of Congress Cataloging-in-Publication Data

Boyle, Doe.

Summer coat, winter coat : the story of a snowshoe hare / by Doe Boyle :
illustrated by Allen Davis.
         p.   cm.
Summary: As the seasons pass, Snowshoe Hare's coat changes from brown to white
and back to brown again, helping her to blend into her habitat and avoid predators
as she searches for food.
        ISBN 1-56899-015-4
1. Hares — Juvenile fiction. [1. Hares — Fiction. 2. Camouflage (Biology) — Fiction.]
I. Davis, Allen. ill. II. Title.
        PZ10.3.B715Su 1993   93-13356
        (E) — dc20   CIP
                                              AC

SUMMER COAT, WINTER COAT

The Story of a Snowshoe Hare

by Doe Boyle

Illustrated by Allen Davis

A Division of Trudy Management Corporation
Norwalk, Connecticut

4

Snowshoe Hare, brown in her summer coat, hides under a willow. She listens to every sound and sniffs the air for every smell. She looks out at the Alaskan grasslands dotted with flowers. Clumps of grasses, lichens and mosses have soaked up the cool spring rain. It is nearly summer.

Outside the cover of the willow, the sunshine warms the green slopes. A golden plover lays its eggs in a nearby hollow. A wheatear and wandering tattler build their summer nests, too. Beneath the tree, in an old grouse wallow, Snowshoe Hare waits.

She nibbles the buds of the willow, but she is still hungry. Tasty green grasses grow nearby, but Snowshoe Hare must stay hidden as the afternoon passes. Safety comes with evening. When shadows fall, she leaves the wallow and hurries to find food.

She pauses at the edge of a thicket. All seems safe, but this is a place of surprise and danger. Snowshoe Hare stretches as tall as she can, checking the grasslands for predators.

A golden eagle wheels slowly overhead, looking for its last meal of the day. Snowshoe Hare must keep still. Not a whisker twitches. The eagle soars away, passing over the far ridge, unaware of Snowshoe Hare. Finally safe, Snowshoe Hare hops to a stream and drinks. She grips the bank with her feet, careful not to slip. Any sudden movement may attract other predators.

Snowshoe Hare lopes in easy bounds, three or four feet long. She eats her fill at the berry patches. A tiny shrew skitters past her, hurrying to feast on tasty grubs. During the long evenings of summer Snowshoe Hare eats and grows. She will get plump for the long Alaskan winter ahead, when food will be hard to find.

By the end of August, the blueberry leaves are scarlet. The aspens, willows and alders are a patchwork of gold and bronze. Fewer hours of sunlight cause Snowshoe Hare's coat to change color also. As the days shorten, she sheds her brown summer hairs. The heavy white hairs of her undercoat grow thickly. They will protect her from the cold and harsh winds of winter.

By early autumn, Snowshoe Hare's coat has become whiter. By winter, she is all white, except for the black tips of her ears. After the first snow falls, Snowshoe Hare blends into the frozen landscape. If she moves carelessly, though, predators will see her.

One evening, Snowshoe Hare pokes her nose under the snow to find food. She misses the scent of a nearby lynx. Snowshoe Hare looks up and suddenly sees him. He is set to pounce.

With an eight-foot leap,
Snowshoe Hare bounds away. The lynx
springs and misses her, but he is not ready to
give up the chase. He follows her trail and pounces
again. Snowshoe Hare runs in wide circles.

She leaps suddenly, changing direction in midair. The lynx plows to a stop. Snowshoe Hare has fooled him. She lands behind him, invisible against a snowdrift. She folds her ears low and waits until the hungry cat slinks away.

Hidden by the shadows of the
snowdrifts, Snowshoe Hare
carefully crosses her frozen world.
Her hind feet are large and covered with
thick hair. They look clumsy, but they carry
her easily over the snow. Like snowshoes,
these big feet pack the snow into deep trails.

Stopping to strip the branch tips of a balsam,
Snowshoe Hare cannot rest for long. Suddenly,
a great horned owl swoops down. Snowshoe
Hare beats one hind foot on the packed snow,
warning other hares of the danger. The hares run
in great leaps, crisscrossing each other's paths.
The owl dives, but misses. Snowshoe Hare darts
to her resting place as morning dawns.

The days lengthen. It is early spring. Snowshoe Hare loses her heavy white winter coat. Soon she is peppered brown again. One last snowstorm comes. Snowshoe Hare stands out against the whiteness. It will be a few weeks before the snow is gone and she blends with the land again.

When the last snow melts, insects begin to buzz. The buds of spring open to the sunshine. One morning in the grouse wallow Snowshoe Hare gives birth to three babies. They are covered with fine, downy brown hair, and their eyes are open. Soon they are on their own. Another summer of growing begins.

About the Snowshoe Hare

The snowshoe hare lives in areas of dense, scrubby vegetation. It spends all of its life out in the open, sheltering only in shallow depressions in the ground or under brush. Females give birth once or twice yearly to 1-7 young (though usually 2-4), nursing them just once daily for only four weeks. Hares live independently, not in groups like rabbits of Europe and Asia. The snowshoe hare is found in the northern United States and Canada. Its fur changes for camouflage purposes and heat conservation in winter. The snowshoe hare is an important link in the food chain, providing meat for carnivores such as lynx, fox and owls.

Glossary

grassland: land or region where grass or sedge is predominate, but may include herbs.

grouse wallow: a shallow, bowl-like depression in the ground, used as a resting or nesting place for grouse and other animals who borrow them.

lichens: a small plant without flowers that grows on rocks, tree trunks or along the ground in clumps.

lynx: a wild animal of the cat family, with long legs, a short tail, and fur in tufts around its mouth and on its ear tips. It is found in the northern United States and Canada, as well as in northern Europe and Asia.

shrew: a tiny mouselike animal with a long, pointed snout, soft brown fur, short rounded ears, and tiny eyes. A fierce fighter, it can kill animals larger than itself. It feeds on insects and worms, eating three times its weight every day.

thicket: a dense growth of shrubbery or small trees.

Points of Interest in this Book

pp. 4-5 willow, lichen and jack-in-the-pulpit.

pp. 6-7 golden plover with eggs; wheatear.

pp. 10-11 daisies and buttercups.

pp. 12-13 golden eagle.

pp. 14-15 bearberries, blueberries, short tail shrew.

pp. 16-17 aspens and bittersweet.